DICK KING-SMITH

Saddlebottom

Illustrated by Robert Bartelt

PUFFIN BOOKS

PUFFIN BOOKS

Published by the Penguin Group
Penguin Books Ltd, 27 Wrights Lane, London W8 5TZ, England
Penguin Putnam Inc., 375 Hudson Street, New York, New York 10014, USA
Penguin Books Australia Ltd, Ringwood, Victoria, Australia
Penguin Books Canada Ltd, 10 Alcorn Avenue, Toronto, Ontario, Canada M4V 3B2
Penguin Books (NZ) Ltd, Private Bag 102902, NSMC, Auckland, New Zealand

Penguin Books Ltd, Registered Offices: Harmondsworth, Middlesex, England

First published by Victor Gollancz Ltd 1985
Published in Puffin Books 1994
This edition with new illustrations published in Puffin Books 1999
7

Typeset in Baskerville

Printed in England by Clays Ltd, St Ives plc

British Library Cataloguing in Publication Data
A CIP catalogue record for this book is available from the British Library

ISBN 0-141-30250-X

PUFFIN BOOKS

Saddlebottom

Dick King-Smith served in the Grenadier Guards during the Second World War, and afterwards spent twenty years as a farmer in Gloucestershire, the county of his birth. Many of his stories are inspired by his farming experiences. Later he taught at a village primary school. His first book, *The Fox Busters*, was published in 1978. Since then he has written a great number of children's books, including *The Sheep-Pig* (winner of the *Guardian* Award and filmed as *Babe*), *Harry's Mad, Noah's Brother, The Hodgeheg, Martin's Mice, Ace, The Cuckoo Child* and *Harriet's Hare* (winner of the Children's Book Award in 1995). At the British Book Awards in 1992 he was voted Children's Author of the Year. He has three children, twelve grandchildren and two great-grandchildren, and lives in a seventeenth-century cottage a short crow's-flight from the house where he was born.

Other books by Dick King-Smith

ACE
THE CUCKOO CHILD
DAGGIE DOGFOOT
DODOS ARE FOREVER
DRAGON BOY
FIND THE WHITE HORSE
THE FOX BUSTERS
HARRY'S MAD
HOW GREEN WAS MY MOUSE
LADY DAISY
MAGNUS POWERMOUSE
MARTIN'S MICE
THE MERMAN
THE MERRYTHOUGHT
THE MOUSE BUTCHER
NOAH'S BROTHER
PADDY'S POT OF GOLD
PRETTY POLLY
THE QUEEN'S NOSE
THE SCHOOLMOUSE
THE SHEEP-PIG
THE STRAY
THE TERRIBLE TRINS
THE TOBY MAN
TREASURE TROVE
TUMBLEWEED
THE WATER HORSE

Contents

CHAPTER 1

Saddlebottom Arrives

All the pigs on the farm were terrible snobs, but Dorothea was the biggest snob of the lot.

If anyone had dared to say this to her face, she would of course have denied it.

'Snobbery,' she would have said, 'is practised only by the middle and lower classes.'

Dorothea's notion of herself as the undoubted leader of farm society was based on three beliefs.

The first was that any pig was immeasurably superior to all other farm livestock, in breeding (and therefore manners), in beauty, and, above all, in

intelligence. Horses and cows, she considered, had limited sense and few brains, and sheep very little of either. Poultry she rated as idiotic.

The second was that her own breed, the Wessex Saddleback, was the noblest pig in the land.

Both these views were shared by the whole herd (Wessex Saddlebacks to a pig) but they were not as happy with Dorothea's third belief, namely that she was the best-bred of them all.

It so happened that there were a number of families in which the sows bore noble titles as names, such as Baroness, Viscountess, or even Marchioness.

But Dorothea's late mother had been a Duchess, and so was she. More, her father had in his day been Supreme Champion at the Royal Wessex Agricultural Show.

'One could hardly be more blue-blooded,' she was fond of saying to the others, looking down her snout at them the while, and she was by no means averse to being addressed as 'Your Grace' by younger or lesser members of the herd, and expected it from such persons as dairy cattle or even, should she be unfortunate enough to happen upon them, common sheep. True, she had to submit to being called plain 'Dorothea' by senior sows, who had known her since she was a piglet, but she much preferred her contemporaries to say 'Duchess', and that in a tone of voice that conveyed a proper respect for her beauty, her brains, and her bloodline. Best of all, they should keep silent and listen to what she had to say. They could learn so much.

One thing she made sure they all learned in due course was that a mating had been arranged for her to a young boar of extremely good family (of almost as ancient a lineage, she let it be known, as her own) and it was perhaps fortunate that her overpowering sense of self-importance, and her drooping ears, prevented her from hearing the comments of the herd.

'It's bad enough,' they said to one another, 'to have

to listen to her holding forth about herself, but just think . . . when she's got a bellyful of little lords and ladies! She's going to be unbearable.' And indeed for the next sixteen weeks it was so.

Dorothea never tired of telling one and all what paragons these piglets would be: how intelligent (they would take after their mother, of course) and how handsome (like their father, the Prince), in the highest tradition of the Wessex breed – black, with a white 'saddle' over the shoulders, and white forelegs.

'Not that you aren't all fairly well-marked,' she would say, 'as one would expect. It's simply that one feels one's own children will attain perfection.' And in the confident anticipation that this would be so, she lay down one night later that summer and gave birth to ten piglets.

Her labour finished, the Duchess rested in the darkness and waited for the first light of dawn and the first sight of her newborn infants She abandoned herself to the pleasure of thinking up names for them, high-sounding patrician names suited to their station.

How honoured the other animals on the farm would be, she thought, imagining the spreading of the news, in stable and cowshed, in sheep-fold and hen-house.

'Have you heard? Her Grace has farrowed!'

'Safely delivered? Praise be!'

'Such a noble lady! Her children are, no doubt, excessively good-looking.'

And nine of them were faultless miniature Wessex Saddlebacks, as like as peas in a pod. The tenth was different, as Dorothea was shortly to find out from the first animal to set eyes upon the litter.

This was not, as she might have hoped, an enviously admiring sow; not even a respectful cow or an awe-struck ewe or, at the very least, a hen made hysterical by such a privilege. It was an old rat, who looked down from a ledge high on the pig-sty wall and said (in a very uncultured voice), 'Yur, thass a rum'un, ain't it, Missus?'

Dorothea snorted with disgust at the effrontery of the creature and said in her most withering tones, 'You will kindly address me in the proper manner.'

'Wass that, then?'

'Your Grace.'

'My Grace?' said the rat. 'All right, if that's what you do fancy. Don't make no odds to I. I just never seed a saddleback like that 'un, and I've seed a few,' and he disappeared into a hole in the wall as Dorothea levered herself to her feet.

'Vulgar wretch!' she grunted. 'Ill-mannered, ill-favoured, and ill-spoken. What can he mean?'

She cast her eye along the rank of tiny plump noblemen and noblewomen so rudely dislodged from

her teats and now wriggling and squeaking in the straw. Inspecting them in turn she saw, as she had every reason to expect, that each was as perfect a little Saddleback as ever graced the land of Wessex. Until, that is, her inspection reached the end of the row and she focused upon the tenth piglet. It was a male, healthy and well-formed; in fact, if anything, the largest of the litter. But its markings! Dorothea's blue blood ran cold in her veins.

The piglet's head was black, yes, and so were its hindlegs. But – oh, what shame! – its forelegs were black also and there was nothing but blackness where the saddle should have been!

'Slipped a bit, 'asn't it, my Grace?' said the rat,

poking his head out again. 'Still, saddles is meant for sitting on.'

Speechless for once, the Duchess Dorothea contemplated the tenth of her highborn children, staring in horror at his little round buttocks. They, and they alone, were white.

'Comic, ain't it?' said the rat. 'You'll 'ave to call 'im Saddlebottom.'

CHAPTER 2

Advice from a Rat

It was really the rat's fault that the name stuck. Dorothea had had no difficulty in deciding upon suitably dignified titles for the rest of her newborn children, such as Lord George, Lord Randolph, Lady Constance, Lady Alexandra, and so forth, but she could not bear to look at the mismarked one, much less be bothered to think up a name for him.

She knew of course that the best-bred Wessex Saddlebacks occasionally produced piglets with too broad or too narrow a saddle, and even sometimes an all-black baby. But the shameful fact that one of her own children should not merely be less than perfect, but actually have a white . . . 'Ugh! One will feed him (with one's eyes shut),' she said to herself, 'but beyond that, one will endeavour not to think about him.'

She had reckoned without the rat.

Whenever he visited Dorothea's sty, which was after each feeding-time – for the crumbs which fell from the rich pig's table – he always made the same enquiry: 'How's little Saddlebottom, my Grace?' he would say.

An angry grunt was the only answer he received, but the other little nobles were quick to latch on to so rude a name for the brother who, they could plainly see, was so different from and therefore so inferior to themselves.

They began by trying to shove him aside and deny him his proper share of their mother's milk, but he was sturdy and determined and held his own. So, as the days went by, they resorted to crueller tactics, cold-shouldering him when he tried to play with them, and passing nasty remarks. They did not address him directly, never in fact spoke to him, but talked about him loudly amongst themselves.

'Jolly bad show,' little Lord Henry would say to his brother, Lord Augustus.

'Lets the side down, doesn't he, what?'

And Lord Augustus, on cue, would reply, 'Who're you talking about, old boy?'

'Why, that Saddlebottom, of course!'

And then they would all run round the sty, squeaking 'Saddlebottom! Saddlebottom!' and fall about laughing.

The little gilts were equally unpleasant, but more subtle.

Lady Katharine and Lady Hermione, for example, would walk slowly and casually past the spot where

Saddlebottom stood alone – for except at feeding-times he always stood alone – and indulge in mutual admiration.

'Your saddle, my dear; how perfectly proportioned it is.'

'My dear! How kind! No more so than yours. Or, for that matter, the saddles of our sisters and brothers.'

'With one exception.'

'Oh my dear, don't speak of it. Mama does not.'

'Poor Mama. The disgrace.'

And the Duchess, listening, said not a word.

So the weeks passed and the piglets grew, and so, too, did Saddlebottom's unhappiness. Not only was he rebuffed by his own kith and kin, who never replied to anything that he said to them, but he also began to imagine that he was a figure of fun to all the other animals on the farm.

Twice daily the dairy herd passed the range of pig-sties on its way to and from the milking-parlour, and there was not one of them, it seemed to Saddlebottom, who at some time did not look over the wall of Dorothea's sty and stare most impolitely at him, often with a snort of what sounded like disgust. He took to sitting in the straw to hide the offending part, but still they stopped to gawk, while the hens and the ducks would fly up on to the wall and cluck and quack in what seemed a most scornful way. Even the sparrows jeered at him, he felt sure, and rows of starlings sat on the electric wires and whistled derisively. Life for Saddlebottom was a misery.

Very early one morning, when the litter was almost eight weeks old, he sat, by himself as usual, puzzling over what his mother had meant the evening before.

'Listen, darlings.' Dorothea had said – and for a moment Saddlebottom's heart had swelled at being included (he thought) in such a term of endearment – 'listen carefully to Mama. Shortly you will all be leaving to make your own way in life and to make your mark, one has no doubt whatsoever, in the Herd Book of the Wessex Saddleback Society. Always remember that you are true aristocrats: above all other farmyard beasts stands the pig; above all other pigs stand the Wessex Saddlebacks; and above all other Wessex Saddlebacks stands each of you, my noble children, all perfectly marked.'

'Not *all*, surely, Mama?' sneered Lady Hermione. 'One could hardly call our dear brother Saddlebottom "perfectly marked".'

Even now the Duchess could not bring herself to speak to or to look directly at the odd-pig-out of her litter, and she had no intention of pronouncing the awful nickname by which he was now known to all.

'He will make himself useful,' she said shortly, and, turning her back upon him, proceeded to outline to the other nine the joys that lay ahead of them, as breeding sows or stock boars, and the honours that she confidently expected them to win at the great agricultural shows.

What did Mama mean, pondered Saddlebottom, as he sat by himself in the outer part of the sty at the night's end and watched the last stars disappear from sight. 'He will make himself useful,' she had said. How?

At that moment the old rat appeared, walking along the top of the wall. Of all the animals he alone ever bothered to speak to Saddlebottom, or rather to say a few words, always the same ones.

'All right then, young 'un?' he said.

Saddlebottom had on all previous occasions replied with a polite 'Yes, thank you,' but now he said, 'No, not really.'

'Wass up then?' said the rat. 'You feeling poorly?' and there was just that note of kindness in his voice that made the piglet decide to unburden himself.

'No,' said Saddlebottom. 'I'm not ill. But I am very unhappy. No one ever speaks to me except you, and when my brothers and sisters talk about me they only say nasty things. They're all going to be champions, but I don't know what's going to become of me.'

'Don't you?' said the rat. 'Ah!'

'My mother said I shall make myself useful. What do you suppose she meant?'

The rat looked down at him consideringly.

'You ever heard tell of pork?' he said.

'No.'

'Or ham?'

'No.'

'Or sausages?'

'No, what are they? What are all these things?'

'I'll tell you, young 'un,' said the rat. 'They're all things as yewmans do eat.'

'Well, what about it?' said Saddlebottom. 'Humans have to eat, I suppose, same as pigs. Or rats. What have all those things to do with me?'

'All those things,' said the rat slowly and deliberately, 'comes out of a pig. Yewmans eats pigs. That's what my Grace meant. That's how you'm a-going to make yourself useful.'

For a time there was silence, broken only by the snores of the Duchess and the crowing of cocks to welcome the new day.

Then, 'Will they eat me very soon?' said Saddlebottom in a small choky voice.

'Bless you, no, young 'un!' said the rat cheerily. 'They'll fill you full of grub first, get you fat. Takes time. You got a good four month to play with yet, I reckon.

'Not that that's going to make you feel a lot happier,' he went on, observing the piglet's even more woebegone face, 'but at least you've got a while to go. You never know your luck.'

'How do you mean? What can I do?'

'Well, look at it like this, young 'un. Your family don't like you, so it ain't going to be no wrench leaving they, and anyway if you do stop, you're for the chop. So it looks to me as though there's only one thing you can do.'

'What's that?' asked Saddlebottom.

'Go,' said the rat. 'Go out into the great wide world and seek your fortune. It can't be no worse than stopping here. Take my advice, young 'un – run away from home. 'Tis the only way to save your bacon.'

CHAPTER 3

Down in the Wood

'Run away from home?' repeated Saddlebottom. He digested the idea for a moment and it both excited and scared him.

'Which way should I go?' he said.

'Haven't got no idea,' said the old rat. 'Never bin beyond the farm buildings meself. It don't make much odds, I should say, barring one thing.'

'What's that?'

'Well, you don't want to stop out in the open. They might come looking for you, see? Tidn't going to be difficult to see a black pig with a white bum in the middle of a green field. You want to keep under cover.'

'Cover?'

'Trees and bushes and that. Make for a wood, I should if I was you – a good thick 'un. You could hide there till you gets your bearings, and there'd be shelter, now winter's coming on, and plenty of stuff about to eat, I daresay. Pigs eats nigh on anything, same as rats.'

Saddlebottom looked doubtful. He pictured himself lost in the middle of a dark wood, cold and tired and hungry, with unknown terrors all about him.

'Course it's up to you,' said the rat. 'You want to lie warm and comfy and stuff yourself full of good food, you stop here. I hear tell they gives you a 'lectric shock afore they cuts your . . .'

'No, no!' cried Saddlebottom. 'I'll go! I'll go straightaway. This morning. Now!' and he ran to the sty door in a fever of anxiety to be off. But of course it was bolted.

'Steady, steady,' said the rat. 'You'll have to wait for one of they yewmans to open that. You pin your ears back, young Saddlebottom, and hark to I. I'll tell 'ee what us'll do.'

So it came about that when a man arrived to feed the Duchess Dorothea and her children that morning, he unbolted the door and was in the act of entering the sty with a bucket of food when he suddenly saw an old rat that stood up on its hindlegs on the wall and

actually bared its yellow teeth at him in the most impudent and provoking manner imaginable. Angrily the man looked about for a stick or stone, but by the time he found something the rat had vanished. Cursing the cheek of the creature, he pulled the door shut and fed the sow and her litter, never noticing that the tally of pushing, shoving, squealing, gobbling little lords and ladies now numbered only nine.

Ten minutes later and almost a mile away, Saddlebottom flumped down exhausted on the crest of a little hill, his heart thudding against his ribs. He had rushed madly through the farmyard and out and away across the fields, his mind empty of every thought save one – to put as much distance as possible between himself and his late home. Blindly he had galloped (for his ears were very floppy), scratching his back under the lowest strands of barbed-wire fences, bouncing off sheep-netting, bursting through hedges, tumbling into ditches, and generally neither looking nor caring where he was going, until the gallop became a canter and the canter slowed, first to a trot and then a walk.

Now he lay and panted, small, fat, puffed and alone in the great wide world of which the rat had spoken. And how great and wide it was, he saw, when at last he had got his breath back and stood up and looked about. It stretched away before him, as far as his eyes could see, in great sweeps of rolling downland, hedgeless, almost featureless, save for an occasional skyline clump of trees. The sky itself seemed enormous, and the piglet felt very exposed as he trotted on again under its huge blue-grey bowl. 'Make for a wood,' the rat had said, and suddenly, as Saddlebottom topped a rise, lo and behold there was one before and below him, and 'a good thick 'un' it looked too, where a runaway piglet might happily hide. He dashed down a steep slope dotted with big domed anthills, and plunged into its shelter.

At first Saddlebottom was too hungry to think of anything but finding food, and then too busy finding it to worry about anything else. But, by the end of his first day, the thrill of escape and the novelty of independence were beginning to wear off. True, his tummy was full of a number of interesting things he had found and gobbled – acorns, beechmast, fungi and various roots, none of whose names he knew but all of whose tastes he liked – but as the light died he began to feel rather cold and very much alone. The wood grew suddenly dark, it seemed, and full of odd noises. Branches groaned, rubbing together high above his head, and nearer, in the undergrowth, there were strange rustlings so that he was relieved to chance upon a big old tree between whose spreading roots was a large hole suitable for a small pig. Into this he crept and lay down to rest. His short legs felt very tired, and his snout was sore from unaccustomed rootling. Above all he was lonely. What he would have given to hear the voice of the rat saying, 'All right then, young 'un?'

He did not know the saying that a friend in need is a friend indeed, but he certainly needed one.

When he woke next morning, after a fitful sleep disturbed by occasional scrabbling noises that seemed to come from within the largely-hollow trunk of the tree, he was greatly cheered – after the first shock of finding it there – to see an extremely friendly face peering in at him.

It was a hairy face, a ginger-coloured face, topped by two rather crumpled ears. It wore a broad lopsided grin and one of its eyes was closed tight in a cheery wink.

Saddlebottom waited a little for the grin to go and the winking eye to open, but the creature's expression remained exactly the same. There was, however, a look in the one open eye which strongly appealed to the piglet. He felt immediately (as very occasionally happens on meeting a total stranger) that here was someone he was going to like very much.

'Hello,' he said. 'What are you?'

'Cat,' said the animal shortly.

'I'm a pig,' said Saddlebottom, coming out of his hole.

'See that,' said the cat. 'Name?'

'I'm known as Saddlebottom.'

The ginger cat walked slowly and carefully all round the piglet.

'Suits you,' he said. 'Bendigo.'

'Sorry?'

'Bendigo. First name.'

'What a very nice name,' said Saddlebottom politely. 'Did your mother give it to you?'

'Yes. Funny old queen she was.'

'Your mother was a Queen? Gosh! Mine was only a Duchess.'

'All she-cats called queens.'

'Oh, I see. But you said "first name". What's your second?'

'They call me Bung-Eye.'

'Oh,' said Saddlebottom. By now he had realized that the wink and the grin were fixed, accounting for the way in which the cat seemed to bite off its words and spit them out of the good side of its face, and he was rather embarrassed by such a direct reference to its deformity.

'Road accident,' said Bendigo Bung-Eye. 'Argument with lorry. Came off worst. Long time ago. Water under bridge. Change subject. You lost?'

'I've run away from home.'

'Why?'

'I don't want to be eaten.'

'Good reason. Sleep all right?'

'Well, not specially. I kept hearing scrabbling noises, like claws scratching on bark . . . Oh . . . Oh dear, was it you?'

'My tree. Live up above.'

'Oh, I'm terribly sorry,' said Saddlebottom. 'I didn't know. I'll find somewhere else to go.'

'No need,' said Bendigo Bung-Eye. 'Welcome to stay. Be company. Bit lonely here.'

'Well, that's jolly kind of you, Mr . . . er . . . Bung-Eye!'

'Bendigo.'

'Oh, can I *really* call you that? Thanks awfully, Bendigo. I would like to stay here for a bit. I need to lie low, you know, in case they come looking for me. And if they do, and you're keeping a look-out too, well, that'll be two pairs of eyes.'

'One-and-a-half,' said the cat, with his permanent wink and grin. 'Come on. Show you round. Have a walk. Nice morning.'

'Oh, it is!' said Saddlebottom happily. 'It is!'

'One thing,' said Bendigo Bung-Eye, as they set off together on a tour of the wood.

'What?'

'"Saddlebottom". Mouthful. Too long. Call you "Sad".'

'Just as you like, Bendigo!' cried Saddlebottom, 'though I don't feel I ever shall be again!'

CHAPTER 4

Dark Days Ahead

A week passed, but nobody came looking for Saddlebottom. Nobody set eyes on him except the animals of the wood, the foxes, the badgers, the squirrels, and many others who watched him walking among the trees with his friend, Bendigo Bung-Eye.

It was a good time of the year for him, for oaks and beeches had shed upon the ground bounty enough for a herd of swine, let alone one small piglet, and Saddlebottom ate well by day (when Bendigo often took a cat-nap) and slept well by night (when Bendigo often took a mouse-snack).

A month more passed, and yet, as he told the cat, he did not miss his family in the least.

'Do you know, Bendigo, the only person that showed me any kindness was a rat!'

'Rat?' said Bendigo Bung-Eye. He passed his tongue across the grinning mouth. 'A fat one, Sad? Must pop down there. Like to meet him.'

'Like to eat him, you mean,' said Saddlebottom. 'No, Bendigo, you really mustn't. It was his idea that I should run away. If it hadn't been for him I should never have met you. Now, I don't know what I should do without you.'

Bendigo Bung-Eye turned his head slightly to look directly at the piglet.

'You'll have to. Soon,' he said.

'Have to what?'

'Do without me. I'm off. Shortly.'

'Off? But Bendigo, I thought you lived here, in the wood, in your tree, always!'

'Not in winter, Sad. Gales. Rain. Frost. Snow. Brrr.'

'Where do you go in the winter, then?'

'Go to town. Adopt a family. Fussed over. Petted. Spoiled. Best of food. Warm and dry. Wait for spring,' and Bendigo Bung-Eye went on to explain how he travelled each year at this time to the nearest country town, and chose a quiet suburban street where the houses looked comfortable; there he would select one that had an adequate garden, no other (male) cats and, above all, no dog. Then, picking his moment (preferably on a night of wind and rain), he

would pose dramatically upon a window-sill, staring yearningly in with his one eye, his paws scrabbling pathetically upon the pane, his mouth open in a soundless mew for help.

'Seldom fails,' he said, though he had to admit there were occasions when his looks (which usually excited sympathy) told against him, especially should he pick upon a household of cat-haters.

'Throw things, sometimes,' he said. 'Funny creatures, humans.'

'I should jolly well think they are!' cried Saddlebottom. 'Eating pigs!'

'Not only pigs, Sad. Cattle, sheep, hens, ducks, geese, turkeys.'

'Cats?'

'No, glad to say. But kill most things. Some for food. Some for fun. Treat cats and dogs special. Family pets. Do no wrong.'

'But surely most cats just stay with their humans always?' said Saddlebottom. 'Why don't you, Bendigo?'

'Like a change. Change of scene. Change of diet. Exercise. Spot of hunting. Fresh air. Independence. Humans very demanding. Constantly wanting affection. Need a break.'

'And you don't always go back to the same house the next winter?'

'Depends. Sometimes sub-standard. Teasing children. No central heating. Uncomfortable bed. Cheap cat-food. Skim milk. Black list. Try elsewhere. Like my comfort. So – winter comes, Bendigo goes.'

Echoing his words, the wind, a cold wind, rose suddenly and whistled through the bare branches overhead. Bendigo Bung-Eye looked skyward.

'Tomorrow,' he added.

'But what about me?' asked Saddlebottom.

'Sorry, Sad,' said Bendigo. 'Must look after Number One. Back in the spring. See you then.'

Saddlebottom spent a bad night. He heard the scratch of claws as the cat left the tree to hunt, and thought with a pang that he would not hear that noise again for ages; months and months of short cold days and long cold nights. Already he felt what he knew he was destined to be – very lonely. And when sleep did come, all it brought was a nightmare in which he was struggling through the wood in deep freezing snow that turned the rest of him white to match his bottom. When he woke with a squeal and looked out of his hole between the roots, it was to see Bendigo Bung-Eye, mouse in mouth, picking his way distastefully over grasses that were glistening with the first frost of winter.

Saddlebottom waited until the cat had finished his breakfast and was cleaning his twisted ginger face with his paws, before asking the question to which he already knew the answer.

'Must you go today, Bendigo?' he said.

'Definitely. Too nippy. By half.'

'Are you going now, this minute?'

'Tonight. Not in daylight. Too dangerous.'

'Dangerous? Why?'

'Got to cross the Plain.'

'The Plain? What's that?'

‘Training ground. Army. Soldiers. With rifles. Shooting. Live ammo. Tanks. Artillery. Mortars. Grenades,’ said Bendigo Bung-Eye, in his voice that was like a burst of machine-gun fire, and he proceeded to give the bewildered pig a short lesson in military matters.

‘But these soldiers,’ said Saddlebottom at the end of it, ‘. . . what are they training to do?’

‘Kill.’

‘What, pigs?’ said Saddlebottom fearfully.

‘No.’

‘What then?’

‘Other soldiers.’

‘To eat them?’

‘No.’

‘Why then? Why should humans want to kill each other?’

‘Not civilized. Like cats are.’

‘Oh. But they don’t do it at night?’

‘Not on the Plain. Not usually. Can’t see in the dark. Like cats can,’ said Bendigo Bung-Eye.

Saddlebottom’s mind was in a whirl at these revelations. Ordinary humans were bad enough, killing cattle and sheep and poultry and pigs, but these soldiers . . . They sounded even more terrible! What a fix he’d be in once Bendigo was gone: he could go back to the farm and be eaten, stay here and freeze to death, or stray out on to the Plain and be shot!

There was only one thing to be done.

'Bendigo', he said. 'When you go, take me with you.'

He looked at his friend's face, imploringly.

'OK. Sad,' said Bendigo Bung-Eye. 'We march tonight!'

CHAPTER 5

Landing in a Hole

'We march tonight!' said the Commanding Officer of the Royal Wessex Rifles. He was sitting in his office at the Regimental Barracks on the other side of the Plain, addressing his Order Group.

This consisted of his Company Commanders, his Intelligence Officer, and, besides them, the Quartermaster (who looked after everyone's stomach), the Padre (who looked after everyone's soul), the Medical Officer (who looked after everyone's feet), and the Regimental Sergeant Major (who looked after everyone).

'It's ages since we did a night exercise,' said the Commanding Officer, and he proceeded to outline his plan for 'Operation Bullseye', which, in a nutshell, required the Royal Wessex Rifles to march very fast indeed for a long way at dead of night right across the Plain. Then, to round things off, the best marksmen in each company (who were to be issued with rifles fitted with night-sights) would be required, weary as they would by then be, to hit a series of targets.

'Each target will be a round white disc,' said the Commanding Officer, 'about the size of a soup-plate. Not easy to hit when you're as fagged out as these chaps will be.'

'That's why you're calling it "Operation Bullseye", Sir,' said the Intelligence Officer.

'Got it first shot,' said the Commanding Officer drily. 'Not for nothing is the Regiment known as "The Sharpshooters". We'll see which company can notch up the highest score.'

All the Company Commanders smiled with quiet confidence and everyone else assumed expressions that were stern and soldierly. The Intelligence Officer in particular tried hard to look intelligent.

Bendigo Bung-Eye on the other hand looked merely puzzled when he came upon the first of the Sharpshooters' targets.

It was near midnight, and he and Saddlebottom had travelled steadily across the Plain. One was confident, taking a well-known route across familiar country, the other excited, nervous on first leaving the safety of the wood but growing in confidence as he marched along behind the waving ginger tail and saw no sign of military monstrosities. He was in fact lost in a happy dream in which he too was adopted by a kindly (vegetarian) family, when he bumped suddenly into the cat.

'Oh, sorry,' said Saddlebottom. 'What's up?' and then as he saw a wooden pole on top of which was fixed something round and white, 'What's that?'

'Don't know,' said Bendigo Bung-Eye, sniffing at the object. 'Smells of man. New to me. Signpost maybe. Seems harmless. Come on.'

They pressed forward across the face of a shallow hillside, dotted with stunted trees and bushes, that bordered a flat-bedded valley, and came shortly on another of the strange things, and then more, until they were in quite a little forest of them.

All of a sudden Bendigo stopped in mid-stride and stood like a statue.

'What . . .?' began Saddlebottom, but was silenced by something between a spit and a snarl. The night was very black and he could see nothing, but after a moment he heard a noise further down the valley, a noise that gradually resolved itself into the sound of footsteps, of many footsteps, of the steps of hundreds and hundreds of feet!

Soldiers! thought Saddlebottom in horror.

He looked at Bendigo Bung-Eye who now lay flat, tail twitching, so he too lay flat, tail tightly curled.

The sounds came steadily nearer along the valley bed until the ground positively shook. And then, just when it seemed that the soldiers would pass the travellers by, a voice shouted an order, and the footsteps all stopped with a thump. Now there were other voices shouting other orders, and then suddenly one enormous bellowing shout:

'FIRE!'

Immediately the air around the two animals was filled with the zing and crack of bullets as they smacked against the trees, through the bushes, into the targets, or ricocheted, whining, off the stones of the hillside.

'Take cover!' yelled Bendigo Bung-Eye, vanishing down a convenient rabbit-burrow. Saddlebottom dashed madly after him, but weeks of gorging on acorns and beechmast had taken their toll, and the rabbit-hole, moreover, narrowed beyond its mouth. Like a cork rammed back into the neck of a bottle, Saddlebottom got so far and no further.

Scrabble as he would, he could not get deeper. Struggle as he might, he could not draw back. He was stuck. As the hail of bullets poured into the hillside, the only bit of him still showing was his behind, a round white disc, about the size of a soup-plate.

Then came the order to cease fire and the shooting stopped as suddenly as it had begun. But, instead of silence, there came to the astonished ears of the Royal Wessex Rifles a strange sound, borne on the

night-wind that blew across the great Plain. One of the targets seemed to be squealing! It was a muffled noise, to be sure, but it was a squeal all right, a squeal of mortal agony!

Agony it might have been, but mortal it was not, as they discovered when they found the source of the squealing, and the Regimental Sergeant Major drew the cork out of the bottle and held it up for his officers' inspection.

Something, a ricocheting bullet or maybe a splinter of rock, had sliced across the exposed part of the squealer, cutting a neat V-shaped mark like the flap of an envelope.

'Would you call that a bullseye?' said the Commanding Officer.

'Oh, no,' said the Intelligence Officer. 'I think it's a pig's bottom.'

'Which needs stitching,' said the Medical Officer. 'It's quite deep, even though it's only a flesh wound.'

'Pretty nice flesh,' said the Quartermaster appraisingly. 'Hardly worth stitching up. He'd be better hung up, and then cut up.'

'Poor little soul,' said the Padre. 'He needs resting and peace, poor chap, of course.'

'He needs roasting, and peas, and apple sauce,' said the Quartermaster.

Privately the Commanding Officer thought this idea had its attractions, but as an animal-loving Englishman it was repugnant to him to consider killing this small innocent appealing-looking creature. As a sportsman it was not cricket, and as a soldier it was unthinkable to shoot prisoners. Anyway, it occurred to him that it would be much more sensible to keep the animal until it grew a great deal bigger. He was particularly fond of a good-sized mature ham. And so, as befitted his title, he issued a series of commands.

The targets were checked and the number of hits scored by each company's marksmen recorded, and then the Royal Wessex Rifles formed up and began the long trek back to barracks.

Behind the rear company marched two riflemen, carrying between them a stretcher upon which lay a

black pig with more than usual white about him, since a quantity of bandage secured a field-dressing to his newly-stitched bottom.

In the concealing darkness a couple of hundred yards behind the stretcher-bearers there marched a ginger cat.

CHAPTER 6

Eat or Be Eaten

Afterwards Saddlebottom could only remember part of what happened that terrible night on the Plain. He remembered the banging, and the panic of sticking in the rabbit-hole, and the awful sudden burning pain in his behind. And he remembered being pulled out and held by one huge human, while another stuck a needle in him. Then there was a big gap in his memory. He knew nothing of the stitching and bandaging of his wound, nor of the interminable journey back into the coming dawn with the long column of soldiers singing as they marched.

Some wag changed the words of one of their songs, and the sound of a thousand voices rolled back over the dopey piglet, dozing unawares upon his stretcher.

'It's a long way to kill a piggy,
It's a long way to go.
It's a long way to kill a piggy,
The smallest pig I know.

Goodbye, little piggy.
Farewell, best of swine.
For I do like sausages for breakfast,
And I wish you were mine.'

When, at long last, he did come properly to his senses and look around, Saddlebottom thought at first that he was back on the farm, for he was lying in a nice thick bed of straw. But when he began to explore, he found that he was in a small room lit only by a barred window set high in one wall. And bars made up one side of this room, thick steel ones set close together, too close, as he found when he tried to squeeze between them.

During the march back across the Plain, it had occurred to the Commanding Officer that, having made the decision to keep the pig, the next question was . . . where? The Royal Wessex Rifles' barracks were not equipped with pig-sties.

As always, when a problem was too much for him, he handed the matter over to the Regimental Sergeant Major.

Accordingly the Regimental Sergeant Major issued the following orders.

The Commanding Officer's pig would be quartered in one of the old detention cells at the rear of the guardroom.

Rations would be drawn for it daily, in the shape of all waste food from the Officers' Mess.

The pig would be fed three times per day, as much

as it could eat. All dung would be transported to the Married Quarters and spread on the Regimental Sergeant Major's vegetable garden.

Further, the pig was to have its own personal attendant. A broad-spoken, stocky, red-faced rifleman, a farm worker before his enlistment in the Royal Wessex Rifles, found himself suddenly promoted, with the resulting improvement in pay and privileges, to the hitherto unknown rank of Corporal-of-Pig.

Thus it was that shortly after Saddlebottom had completed his exploration of his prison, he heard the clang of an outer door, and then smelt a smell so glorious that he forgot his troubles and began to squeal loudly with anticipation. And when the figure of a soldier appeared, Saddlebottom forgot also that soldiers were, in his short experience, terrifying creatures, and saw only the huge tin pan which the man carried and, having opened the barred door of the cell, set down upon its floor. Oh, what a blissful banquet for a hungry pig!

There was cold porridge and soggy cornflakes; smears of egg and snippets of kipper; fillets of fish-finger and lumps of bread, rich with grease or flavoured with marmalade or jam or honey; and blobs of tomatoey baked beans, and milk-dregs, and tea-leaves, and coffee-grounds, and even (whisper it)

ham-fat and *bacon-rinds* – all mixed up into the most beautiful slosh that a pig could wish to slabber.

When at last he had licked the pan shiningly clean, there were further pleasures in store. The soldier who had brought the food first rubbed his ears deliciously with expert fingers, talking to him the while in the most soothing manner, and then brushed him all over (except for his bandaged backside), cleaned up the floor most carefully, and shook up the thick dry straw to make an inviting bed on which a blown-out pig might sleep off so magnificent a meal.

But after no more than forty winks, it seemed to

Saddlebottom, the man was back with another huge panful. And again, in the evening, as the Regimental Sergeant Major had decreed, the pan was filled (and emptied) for the third time.

Whether it was due to the strain of the previous twenty-four hours, or to rather a lot of toasted cheese that formed part of the third big meal, Saddlebottom's first night as the guest of the Royal Wessex Rifles was a troubled one. As on his last night in the wood, he had a nightmare.

He began by dreaming about his friend, Bendigo Bung-Eye, and that was nice – to see that winking grinning face again. But then the dream-face began to change. Its shut eye opened and its grin disappeared, and it became longer and thinner, and grey instead of ginger, until it was the face of the old rat that said, with an expression of great sadness, 'Yewmans eats pigs,' before it changed once again. This time the face became human, the face of a soldier, in uniform, with a crown and star on either shoulder of that uniform. Beneath the neat clipped military moustache, the mouth began to open, wider, wider . . . 'NO!' squealed Saddlebottom. 'Don't eat me! Please don't!'

CHAPTER 7

Badge on the Behind

Later, just before he dropped off to sleep again, he wondered for a moment if the rat could possibly have been wrong about the habits of humans. These soldiers seemed awfully nice. At the sound of his squealing the Sergeant and the Lance-Corporal and the six riflemen of the Guard had all come running from the guardroom to find out what the matter was, and to comfort him with soothing words and by scratching his back and tickling his ears, and then by bringing him leftovers from their supper and generally making a fuss of him.

And next day everyone seemed very kind. The Corporal-of-Pig brought him marvellous meals again, and a number of other more important-looking soldiers came to the cell to visit him, and to rub and pat him, and talk to him in what sounded a very pleasant way. One of them, Saddlebottom could see when the man bent down to him, did indeed have a crown and star on either shoulder and a neat clipped military moustache, but somehow he didn't look like a pig-eater.

'Polishing off his grub, is he?' said the Commanding Officer.

'Sir!' said the Corporal-of-Pig, coming smartly to attention with a stamp of his foot that shook the

concrete floor. Perhaps he's got an itch, thought Saddlebottom, and this reminded him that his bottom felt tickly and he began to rub it against the bars.

The tickliness, though he did not know it, was a sign that his wound was healing nicely, and indeed this was confirmed the very next day when the Medical Officer came to examine it. The Padre, the Intelligence Officer and the Regimental Sergeant Major had all come along with him, and they watched as the bandages were removed. Saddlebottom stood perfectly still and did not struggle or try to move away, because something told him that once again here was a human trying to help him.

'Bless him!' said the Padre.

The Intelligence Officer looked puzzled. 'I thought that was your job,' he said.

The bandages off, the Medical Officer examined the injury, that neat V-shaped mark like the flap of an envelope.

'Clean as a whistle,' he said. 'Those stitches can come out in a few days, though he'll carry the scar till his dying day – which'll be in a couple of months, I should say.'

'Oh Death, where is thy sting?' said the Padre solemnly.

'Curious that the wound should be that precise

shape,' said the Medical Officer. 'D'you all see what I'm getting at?'

'Oh Grave, where is thy victory?' said the Padre. 'It's a V for Victory.'

'It looks like the flap of an envelope,' said the Intelligence Officer.

The Medical Officer raised his eyebrows in a pained way.

'No, no,' he said. 'What I meant was . . . oh tell 'em, Sar'Major.'

'Sir!' said the Regimental Sergeant Major loudly. 'The injury, Sir, resembles the single chevron carried as a badge of rank on the upper sleeve of the uniform of the lowest non-commissioned rank. Sir!'

The Intelligence Officer looked puzzled.

'It looks to me like a Lance-Corporal's stripe,' he said.

And thus it was that the pig which the Duchess Dorothea had not bothered to give even one name of his own acquired a second one, for word soon went round the barracks that the Commanding Officer's pig had been promoted Lance-Corporal, and, to save the trouble of saying that in full, everyone called him Lance.

'How's old Lance getting on?' men would ask the Corporal-of-Pig, and his progress was a matter of general interest in the Officers' Mess.

'Fine little chap,' they said. 'Settled in well,' and there were many visits to the old detention cells to see such an apparently contented prisoner.

But, despite outward appearances, Lance-Corporal Saddlebottom was by no means as happy as the Regiment thought. He was well fed – no doubt of that – superbly fed, looked after with care and treated with the utmost kindness, but no day passed when he did not recall the old rat's words.

'They'll fill you full of grub first, get you fat. Takes time.'

How long, thought Saddlebottom, and no day passed when he did not make a firm resolution to try to refuse most of the food they lavished on him, only eating just a little bit, enough to keep body and soul together, and so prolonging his expectation of life in the hope that some miracle might save him.

But somehow, when each delicious meal arrived, eating just a little bit led to eating just a little bit more, and before you could say, 'Royal Wessex Rifles', that led to eating the lot.

So that, a couple of weeks after Operation Bullseye, it was a very different-looking pig that the Commanding Officer, accompanied by the Regimental Sergeant Major, came to inspect – a pig that bore little resemblance to the shocked and bleeding victim that the stretcher-bearers had carried across the Plain.

'By Jove,' said the Commanding Officer, scratching Saddlebottom's ever-broadening back with his cane, 'our honorary Lance-Corporal is blowing up like a balloon, eh, Sar'Major?'

'Sir!' barked the Regimental Sergeant Major.

'No trouble, is he?'

'Model prisoner, Sir.'

'H'm,' said the Commanding Officer. He put his cane under his arm and pulled reflectively at his moustache. 'Well, I'm afraid I can't consider any remission of sentence for good behaviour.'

'Ha, ha, no, Sir.'

A silence fell.

'Shame really, Sir,' said the Regimental Sergeant Major, in a voice much softer than his customary shout. He took his pace-stick from under his arm and tickled the pig with the sharp brass point of it, gently. Saddlebottom squirmed in silent pleasure.

'He's a nice sort of animal,' said the Regimental Sergeant Major. 'Seems a pity to eat him.'

'I agree,' said the Commanding Officer. 'But what else can you do with a pig?'

CHAPTER 8

Oh, What a Sound!

That night the Corporal-of-Pig brought Saddlebottom a particularly delicious supper. A large salmon destined for the Officers' Mess had taken so long to arrive from the Lowlands of Scotland that it had become high, and the officers had turned up their noses at it. Saddlebottom put his down into it and kept it down till there was nothing left, not even a single fish-scale.

Now all was quiet. The Corporal-of-Pig had tidied everything up and gone, the riflemen on guard duty had looked in to say good-night to Lance and give him a last pat, and it was time for Lights Out. Lance-Corporal Saddlebottom lay in his deep straw bed.

He felt very full – of food and of woe.

I should be happy, he thought, after all the attention and kindness I get, but to tell the truth I just feel sad.

'I'm sad,' he said out loud.

'Sad?' said a voice in reply, and he started up in surprise at this strange echo that seemed to come from the passageway beyond the bars of his cell. Then he saw in the gloom one gleaming eye!

'Bendigo!' he gasped. 'Is it you?'

'Definitely,' said Bendigo Bung-Eye. 'Promise you. Cross my heart. Hope to die.'

'Oh, don't say that to me!' cried Saddlebottom.

'Sorry, Sad. Wasn't thinking. How's life?'

'All right at present, Bendigo. It's the future I'm worried about. But anyway you don't want to hear about my troubles – it's a lovely surprise to see you again – how did you get in here?'

'Followed your supper. Smelt good. Nice bit of fish?'

'Yes, it was super . . . Oh, I'm sorry, you could have had some if I'd known . . . I didn't see you. I was so busy eating and then I was so full I had to go and lie down. Oh, I am a greedy pig! Bendigo, are you hungry?'

'No,' said Bendigo Bung-Eye. He came forward and squeezed himself through the bars of the cell, with some difficulty.

'You look awfully . . . well,' said Saddlebottom. 'Tell me, what happened to you after the shooting?'

'Followed you in. Had a look round. Decided to join up. Short-term enlistment. Change from Civvy Street.'

'You mean the soldiers have adopted you?'

'Made myself useful. Rat patrol. Heavy casualties. No prisoners taken. Mentioned in despatches. Taken on strength.'

'Oh, that's smashing, isn't it! Where are you living?'

'Cook-house. Good billet. Attached to Sergeant-Cook. Very attached.' Saddlebottom looked fondly at his friend, winking and grinning as ever, and could see a great change from the scraggy unkempt animal that he had met in the wood not all that long ago. Bendigo Bung-Eye was positively tubby his ginger coat gleaming with health.

'You've put on a lot of weight,' said Saddlebottom.

'So've you.'

'I know, I know. I can't seem to stop eating. In fact I've eaten so much tonight, I've got a job to keep my eyes open.'

Bendigo Bung-Eye settled himself comfortably against the plump warm cushion of the pig's stomach. 'Shut 'em,' he said, and closed his only one.

Once it was established that the Sergeant-Cook's cat liked to visit the Colonel's pig, each relieving guard ensured that in daytime the connecting door between the cells and the guardroom was left ajar. And it was through this gateway to the outside world that Saddlebottom first heard that sound which was to play such a part in his life.

It was the following Sunday morning, and he had been lying stretched out in the straw, listening lazily to Bendigo Bung-Eye's descriptions of the joys of the life of a cook-house cat, when the first distant thumping reached his ears. That's all it was to begin with, just a distant rapid thump-thump-thump and a kind of dull roar of noise.

But then, as the Band of the Royal Wessex Rifles drew nearer, marching back to barracks at the head of the Regiment on its return from Church Parade, Saddlebottom began to distinguish the various sounds that went to make the whole. What was causing them he had no idea, but what they sounded like was immediately apparent to him, and he thought it the most thrilling noise he had ever heard.

The shrilling of the cornets was the squealing of hungry piglets, the wail of the trombones was the yelling of famished porkers, the blare of the euphoniums was the grunting of starving sows, and the metallic clash of the cymbals was the setting down of great buckets of scrumptious food before the ravening, slavering herd. And permeating and controlling all these strains, beating out that snappy 150-paces-to-the-minute rhythm, at which every rifle regiment marches, were the drums, the high hammering of the kettle-drums and the thunderous sonorous boom of the big bass drum.

The Band was playing the Regimental March

'Weeds be in the mangel-wurzels,
Hoe! Boys! Hoe!'

and by the time they swept in through the barrack gates and past the guardroom, and the full blast of the music crashed into the little cell, Saddlebottom was half crazy with excitement.

Impelled by some force he did not understand and without realizing at all what he was doing, he marched madly around the perimeter of his prison. His blood raced, his heart hammered, and as he gasped for breath his mouth hung open in a soundless scream. Only when, after a warning double-thump by the bass- drummer, the Band at last fell silent and a single distant voice could be heard dismissing the parade, did Lance-Corporal Saddlebottom come to a panting halt.

'Oh, Bendigo!' he said. 'Oh, whatever was that?'

'Regimental Band,' said Bendigo Bung-Eye. 'Soldiers making noises. Blowing things. Banging things. Filthy row.'

'Oh no!' cried Saddlebottom. 'It was a marvellous, marvellous sound. I just felt I'd give anything to march with them!'

Bendigo looked at his friend's face, consideringly. He put his paw up and pulled reflectively at his whiskers.

'March with them, eh, Sad?' he said. 'That's an idea.'

'Oh if I could, I think I'd die happy.'

'You might live happy,' said Bendigo Bung-Eye.

CHAPTER 9

Tape-recorder Trial

By the end of that day they had worked out a plan. Or rather Bendigo Bung-Eye had worked it out while Saddlebottom listened with growing excitement. Like all the best plans it was simple and straightforward. All that was needed was for the Band to play again and for an officer with a few brains (so, *not* the Intelligence Officer) to witness Saddlebottom's reaction to the music.

Thus it came about on the following Sunday morning that the Corporal-of-Pig (to his great surprise) found that Lance (by an enormous effort of will) had not eaten his breakfast.

Informed of this, the Regimental Sergeant Major came, before Church Parade, to inspect the Commanding Officer's pig for himself, and he found the food was indeed untouched, and that the animal, far from approaching the bars of the cell for a back-scratch in its usual friendly manner, lay looking listless and dispirited. Saddlebottom even managed a rather theatrical groan.

The Regimental Sergeant Major marched himself in front of the Medical Officer.

'Hello, what's the problem, Sar'Major?' said the

Medical Officer. 'Surely *you*'ve not got trouble with your feet?'

'Ha, ha, no, Sir. It's the Commanding Officer's pig, Sir. Reported sick this morning, Sir, rations untouched. Animal appears to be unfit for duty.'

'Oh. Well, thanks for letting me know, Sar'Major. I'll stroll down later on and take a look at him.'

As luck would have it, the Medical Officer was not required to attend Church Parade and had no specific duties of a Sunday morning, so he tended to sit over his breakfast with the newspapers. Thus it was not until nearly midday that he strolled down.

He made his way to the cell block, and there indeed was a prostrate pig, its food untasted.

'What's up then, old chap?' he said and, as though in answer, Saddlebottom, playing for time, began a series of small moaning noises. Then, in the nick of time, he heard the distant sound of the Band as the Regiment marched off from church.

No Wessex Saddleback can actually prick up its ears, but the Medical Officer was left in no doubt of the animal's immediate alertness. What had seemed a bed-ridden pig suddenly opened its eyes, raised its head, leaped to its feet, stood for an instant tense and quivering, and then, as though at an unheard word of command, began to walk smartly round and round the cell.

The Medical Officer was a Welshman, a foreigner

among the stolid West-countrymen of the Royal Wessex Rifles, and music was meat and drink to him. To his amazement he noticed that the pig's response to the sound of the approaching Band was not simply one of nervous excitement: the creature was marching, actually marching, in perfect time with the music!

Against the now deafening noise of the passing Band the Medical Officer shouted wildly for the Sergeant of the Guard, who came running in from the guardroom, sub-machine-gun at the ready, thinking that the Commanding Officer's pig had turned vicious.

'Look at that,' said the Medical Officer.

Together they stared at the marching pig.

'He's keeping step, Sir,' said the Sergeant of the Guard. 'He's keeping in step with the music!'

Then the music stopped, and the pig stopped. He stood, flanks heaving, eyes glazed and staring like one bewitched.

'I wonder . . .' said the Medical Officer softly.

'Sir?'

'Sergeant. Is there somewhere we could put him where he's got room to move? Don't want him getting loose and running around barracks, but is there somewhere he could stretch his legs?'

'Well, Sir . . . there's the old exercise yard.'

At the rear of the guardroom, behind the cell block, was a walled area the size of a cricket pitch. It was never used now, but many years ago prisoners under arrest had been allowed a few moments there each day to get some fresh air.

'Let's have a look at it,' said the Medical Officer, and having seen it, said, 'Yes, this will do. But how are we going to get him here from the cell?'

'He'll follow the Corporal-of-Pig when he brings his food, Sir, I should think. Go anywhere if there's a bucket of grub in front of him, Lance will.'

'But he's off his food.'

'Oh yes, Sir, I was forgetting.'

However, when they walked back to the cell the trough was licked clean.

'Blimey,' said the Sergeant of the Guard. 'His next meal's due shortly.'

'I want it postponed,' said the Medical Officer. 'Order the Corporal-of-Pig to report to you with the next meal at 2245 hours. Tell off a couple of riflemen as prisoner's escort, and march Lance to the exercise yard and feed him there. I want him on parade in that yard at 2300 hours, ready for the Commanding Officer's inspection.'

Hearing of this plan, the Regimental Sergeant Major marched himself to the exercise yard at 2250 hours, satisfied himself that the pig was in position, noted that the day's second meal had been consumed, and dismissed the Corporal-of-Pig and the prisoner's escort.

At 2300 hours precisely the Commanding Officer arrived, accompanied by the Medical Officer, the Intelligence Officer, and the Bandmaster who was carrying a large tape-recorder.

The Regimental Sergeant Major took two paces forward, stamped his foot fit to crack the concrete, and in a voice that brought birds fluttering stunned from the skies shouted, 'Permission to join pig inspection, Sir!'

'By all means, Sar'Major,' said the Commanding Officer. 'We're about to conduct a little experiment,' and to the Bandmaster he said, 'Switch the thing on, please.'

The Bandmaster turned the volume control up full and pressed a switch, and out from the machine crashed the opening bars of

> 'Weeds be in the mangel-wurzels,
> Hoe! Boys! Hoe!'

Now, with room to move, Saddlebottom's performance was vastly more impressive. Tail curled smartly tight, head held proudly high, he swung away down the exercise yard, stepping precisely to the music. As he approached the wall at the far end, 'About Turn!' shouted the Regimental Sergeant Major automatically, and round the pig spun, light on his feet as any cat, the one-eyed cat for example that lay on the top of the wall watching the performance.

'See what I mean, Colonel?' said the Medical Officer with pride.

'Amazing,' said the Commanding Officer in amazement.

'Delightful,' said the Bandmaster in delight.

'Mystifying,' said the Intelligence Officer in mystification.

After a while, the Commanding Officer said, 'Turn it off, please, Bandmaster.' The music stopped. The pig stopped. The inspection party stood speechless. Simultaneously the same thought had occurred to all of them (except the Intelligence Officer).

'Other regiments have them,' said the Commanding Officer slowly.

'Goats,' said the Medical Officer. 'Shetland ponies. Irish wolfhounds.'

'And they couldn't march in strict tempo like that,' said the Bandmaster.

'But a pig . . .' said the Commanding Officer doubtfully. 'And such an oddly-marked one at that.'

As always, when a problem was too much for him, he handed the matter over to the Regimental Sergeant Major.

'What kind of pig is it, Sar'Major?'

'Wessex Saddleback, Sir,' said the Regimental Sergeant Major, who came of country stock. 'Improperly marked, but definitely a Wessex Saddleback, Sir.'

'Wessex Saddleback, eh?' said the Intelligence Officer. 'I say, what a coincidence. I mean, we're the Wessex Rifles.'

'And speaking of the animal's markings, Sir,' went on the Regimental Sergeant Major . . .

'Yes?' said the Commanding Officer.

'With respect, Sir, it occurs to me that the fact of the animal possessing a white backside might render him particularly suitable – in view of the regimental motto, Sir.'

The regimental motto was

Vestigia nulla retrorsum

a Latin phrase meaning 'no going back', or, in other words, 'no retreat in the face of the foe'.

'Marching behind an animal marked in this

manner, Sir, would, if I might suggest, act as a constant reminder to the Regiment of their duty never to turn their backsides to the enemy, Sir.'

The Commanding Officer looked at the Medical Officer, and the Medical Officer looked at the Bandmaster, and they all grinned.

Suddenly the Intelligence Officer, who throughout the whole conversation had looked extremely puzzled, broke into a smile.

'I say!' he said. 'I've just had a jolly fine idea. That pig would make a good mascot!'

CHAPTER 10

Triumph on the Square

Now there began for Saddlebottom a period of intensive training.

Though he was to be enrolled as a member of the Band and would therefore come under the orders of the Bandmaster, it was the Regimental Sergeant Major who insisted upon personally supervising a basic drill course for the new recruit. As often as his duties permitted he would come to the exercise yard (to which Saddlebottom now went very willingly without the inducement of food) accompanied by a bandsman to operate the tape-recorder; and before

the week was out he had trained the pig to respond to three commands – 'Quick March', 'About Turn', and 'Halt!'.

The first and last of these he taught by having the music switched on or off just before giving the order; and he shouted, 'About Turn!' as before, at the exact moment when Saddlebottom's only altenative to turning about was to walk straight into the wall.

Finally, when the Regimental Sergeant Major was satisfied that these three commands had become thoroughly ingrained in the mind of the recruit, he tried giving them without the music. To his great satisfaction the pig responded as smartly as ever.

By the end of another week the Regimental Sergeant Major held a private pig's passing-out parade, pronounced himself satisfied, and handed

over responsibility to the Bandmaster. Saddlebottom would continue, for his own comfort, to be billeted in the detention block, but his days as a prisoner were over. Above his door the Pioneer Sergeant fitted a beautiful piece of varnished board. On it was inscribed in gold lettering

2622809 L/Cpl. Pig, W.S.
(the initials stood for his breed)
'Lance'
Att. Regtl. Band.
Royal Wessex Rifles.

The condemned cell had become the private quarters of the Regimental Mascot.

Saddlebottom felt extremely pleased with life. He had no way of telling what was in store for him but he was pretty confident about what was not. The soldiers were not going to eat him, he felt sure. That big one, the one who had pulled him out of the rabbit-hole, had seemed very pleased that afternoon, scratching him with his pointed stick and talking to him quite softly in his deep rumbly voice.

'He's nice,' said Saddlebottom afterwards to Bendigo Bung-Eye, who had as usual lain on top of the wall and cast an eye on the proceedings. 'But he doesn't half shout at me. Perhaps he thinks I'm deaf.'

'All soldiers shout,' said Bendigo Bung-Eye. 'Shout. Stamp feet. March about. Swing arms.' He yawned and curled himself more comfortably in the fresh clean straw. 'Hyperactive,' he said. 'That's their trouble. Can't relax,' and he went to sleep.

The next morning the Bandmaster came to the detention block, accompanied by the Corporal-of-Pig. Realizing that the pig would have to be restrained in an area as big as the barrack square, the Bandmaster had had a kind of harness made from an old set of the strappings which are used to attach bass drums to bass-drummers.

'Try it on him,' he said to the Corporal-of-Pig.

Saddlebottom made no objection as the harness was fitted on him. Anything the Corporal-of-Pig did was fine with him.

Now came an historic moment as for the first time Saddlebottom set trotter on the barrack square of the Royal Wessex Rifles.

The square was deserted, except for the Band, standing at ease at the far end, for the bulk of the Regiment was out of barracks on field training or at the rifle ranges; but nonetheless there were four pairs of eyes (and one single one) watching that historic moment with interest and anxiety.

From the windows of their respective offices the Medical Officer and the Regimental Sergeant Major looked out, one at his patient, one at his pupil; in the great front door of the Officers' Mess stood the Commanding Officer, pulling nervously at his neat clipped military moustache, while at an upper window the Padre offered a short prayer; and outside the cook-house the Sergeant-Cook's cat sat purring loudly, partly because he had just breakfasted unusually well and partly at the sight of his friend marching smartly across the square, at the side of the Corporal-of-Pig, towards the waiting Band.

'Halt!' shouted the Bandmaster, and they halted. About Turn!" and they turned about.

Then the bandsmen made ready. Brass instruments were poised for blowing, drumsticks were lifted for tattooing and cymbals raised for clashing. The bass-drummer hoisted on to his big leopardskin-covered chest the big bass drum.

Three figures took station in front of the ranks of musicians, the Drum-Major with his ceremonial staff and, beside him, the Corporal-of-Pig and his charge, each rigidly at attention – heels together, chins in, chests out, shoulders back.

Now the watchers heard a brand-new command ring out.

'Band and Mascot!' shouted the Bandmaster. 'By the Right. Quick March!' And away they went to the roaring strains of another favourite number in the repertoire of that rurally recruited regiment

'Mow the enemy down, Lads!'

And as they saw how sharply the pig stepped out,

how precisely he marched to the beat, how proudly he bore himself in a truly soldierly manner, broad grins spread across the faces of four of the watchers. As for the fifth, his grin was fixed. He looked like a cat that has eaten the cream (which is just what he had done).

'Very good,' he said. He sat and licked his chops and stared as the Band went by him at the usual rattling pace; at their head the Regimental Mascot, his black head looking neither to left nor to right, the Lance-Corporal's stripe of his wound showing clearly against the whiteness of his fat bottom.

'Very good,' said Bendigo Bung-Eye again, and he rose and stretched himself luxuriously before padding back into the cook-house.

CHAPTER 11

Off to the Show

The winter months progressed and Saddlebottom progressed with them. By Christmas the pig harness was a thing of the past, so accustomed had he become to marching always at the side of the Corporal-of-Pig, his right ear exactly level with the man's left knee.

Responding to the three first-learned commands was second nature to him now, and he had learned to obey several more. The Corporal-of-Pig carried a long stick and at the command 'Right Turn!' would touch the pig with it on the left shoulder. To turn him in the opposite direction he touched the other shoulder, while a tap of the stick between the shoulder-blades signified 'Mark Time!'.

At first the Corporal-of-Pig used a broom handle, but this was patently not suitable for formal occasions and eventually a splendid silver-headed malacca cane was commandeered from the Regimental Museum.

And then, at last, there came a day in early springtime when the Corporal-of-Pig, armed with this ceremonial stave, and with the Regimental Mascot stiffly at attention by his side, stood at the head of the Regiment as they prepared to march past no less a person than the General Officer Commanding The Wessex Division.

What a sight Saddlebottom was! The winter of good feeding and healthy exercise had turned him from a podgy young porker to a magnificent mature animal, long and muscular and heavier far than any

man on parade, his well-brushed coat gleaming with oil, his polished trotters twinkling in the spring sunshine. Behind him the riflemen marched as they had never marched before, every heart swelling with pride, every eye fixed upon that white bottom, the constant reminder that the Sharpshooters would never turn their backs on the enemy.

And, as they swept past the saluting base and the Commanding Officer gave the order 'Royal Wessex Rifles, Eyes Right!', the merest tap of the silver-headed malacca cane on his left ear brought Saddlebottom's head snapping round.

'Absolutely amazing!' said the General afterwards, over lunch in the Officers' Mess. 'As well-drilled as any guardsman!'

'We're rather proud of our training programmes, Sir,' said the Commanding Officer modestly.

'But a pig . . .!'said the General, shaking his head in disbelief. He looked out of the dining-room windows and saw a ginger cat sitting on the sill outside. It seemed to be winking. The General jerked his thumb at it.

'What have you trained that to do?' he said. 'Play the fiddle?'

Everyone laughed dutifully, and even the cat seemed to be grinning.

'Grub looked good,' said Bendigo Bung-Eye that

evening. 'Smoked salmon. Roast duck. Crème brûlée. Ripe Stilton. Mouth watered.'

'I know,' said Saddlebottom. 'After all, I get their leftovers.'

The Corporal-of-Pig, moreover, took a great deal of trouble with the preparation of Saddlebottom's food, discarding any material which he did not consider to be of top quality, and always heating the meal before serving it.

'I've certainly got no complaints,' said Saddlebottom. 'But then I shouldn't think you have either, Bendigo. I bet you do jolly well in the cookhouse. You'll miss it, won't you?'

'Miss it, Sad?'

'Well, I remember what you said. You like a change at this time of year, now that summer's coming. A change of scene, a change of diet, some exercise and independence. Humans can be very demanding, you said, so you'll be needing a break. When are you going back to the wood?'

Bendigo Bung-Eye looked away. He appeared a trifle embarrassed.

'Changed my mind,' he said. 'Not getting any younger. Long way to go. No one to talk to. Might stay on.'

'Oh good,' said Saddlebottom. 'I am glad. What a nice surprise!'

*

'What a nice surprise!' said the Commanding Officer at about the same moment. The General was about to leave, his large car drawn up outside the Mess, but first he had taken the Commanding Officer aside, out of earshot of the other officers, and spoken a few words to him.

And just before he was driven away, the General put his head out of the rear window and said, 'You'll hear officially before long, Billy, but I thought you'd like to know in advance. Top secret, mind. Just between you and me.'

'Absolutely, Sir,' said the Commanding Officer. 'Wouldn't dream of telling a soul.'

Which made it all the more surprising that within an hour or so there wasn't a single person in barracks (except Saddlebottom and Bendigo Bung-Eye) who had not heard the news about the Colonel-in-Chief of the Regiment.

The Colonel-in-Chief of the Royal Wessex Rifles was a Royal Lady (and another of the many honorary positions which she held was that of President of the Royal Wessex Agricultural Society).

The news was this: as President, the Royal Lady was to open, in early June, the Agricultural Society's 60th Annual Show and she had expressly requested that the military band chosen to provide the customary musical march should be that of her own regiment, the Royal Wessex Rifles.

‘’Course she doesn’t know about the pig, Billy,’ the General had said, ‘but she’s fond of animals.’

‘I hope she’ll approve of him, Sir,’ said the Commanding Officer.

‘She’ll be tickled pink!’ said the General, winding up the window. ‘Drive on!’

Now began a period of furious activity for the Band.

April was already more than half gone, and everyone knew that in no more than six weeks they would be on parade, before the Royal Lady, before the thousands of people at the Show ground, before the millions who would watch on their television screens. For the honour of the Regiment, everything must be perfectly done.

Over and over again the bandsmen practised the chosen pieces of music, over and over again they marched and counter-marched upon the barrack square. Saddlebottom even learned a new drill movement, not known in any army training manual – the ‘Sit To Attention’ (one tap of the cane on his white behind). And finally he was issued with a full-dress uniform (a fine leather collar made from an officer’s Sam Browne belt, with a brass identity disc attached bearing his number, rank and name).

‘How d’you like this then, Bendigo!’ he said

proudly. 'Pretty smart, don't you think? I tell you what – Mama would never recognize me now!'

But she did.

It was, at long last, the evening before the opening day of the Royal Wessex Agricultural Society's 60th Annual Show, and already the pens and sheds on the Show Ground were filled with hundreds of magnificent specimens of the finest pedigree livestock in the country.

There were horses and ponies of every shape and size, dairy cows and beef cattle of every known type, and sheep, goats and poultry; and, of course, pigs. Large White and Landrace, Berkshire and Tamworth, Gloucester Old Spots and Wessex Saddleback – they mostly lay and grunted in the deep, clean wood-shavings of their pens, waiting for the morrow and the chance to prove themselves supreme in their breed. Several, however, were being exercised in the evening sunshine, their pigmen in attendance, and one of these, a very large beautifully-marked Wessex Saddleback sow, was making her stately way across the grass of the pig-ring when a convoy of army trucks drove by. As the last vehicle passed the Duchess Dorothea, a droop-eared head suddenly appeared over its tail-gate and a loud excited voice yelled, 'Mama! Mama!'

Who can it be, wondered Dorothea – Lord Henry,

Lord Randolph, Lord Augustus? How splendid! Between us we may sweep the board – Supreme Champion Sow and Supreme Champion Boar – and she quickened her pace towards the now stationary truck.

As she drew nearer, the tail-gate was lowered, a soldier placed a wooden ramp against the rear of the vehicle, and down the ramp walked a ginger cat, followed by a large black boar.

'It's a Large Black boar,' said Dorothea to herself in disappointment. 'Why on earth was it squealing at me?' And then, as the soldier tapped it on one shoulder with a long silver-headed cane, the animal turned sideways to her. It had the whitest of white bottoms.

Horrified, the Duchess turned and hastened away, her pigman hurrying to keep up with her, a last cry of 'Mama!' pursuing her as she made for the safety of her pen.

'My dear,' said her neighbour, 'don't tell me you are related to that creature?'

'What a perfectly ridiculous idea,' said the Duchess Dorothea loftily. 'And you will kindly address me as "Your Grace".'

Night fell, and at last all was quiet in the Show Ground. The thousands of animals slept, more or less soundly, in their pens, and their human attendants dossed down beside them and snatched what rest they could. A brilliant moon shone upon the great tented camp and showed a scene of almost total stillness. Only one thing moved, for Bendigo Bung-Eye did not feel in the least bit sleepy.

Once everyone was settled – Saddlebottom on a straw bed in the back of the truck, the bandsmen bivouacked all about it – Bendigo set off in search of the Duchess Dorothea. He had not planned anything particular to say to her. He was simply nosy, wanting to see the mother of his friend, a mother who before his very eye had turned her back upon that cry of 'Mama!' and hurried away in the opposite direction. But then perhaps she had not recognized her son? It must be difficult to see with ears like that. Bendigo felt intensely curious about her.

Finding the pig lines was easy – his sense of smell told him where to go – but, once there, he had need of his keen night sight to distinguish one breed from another. At last he came to the pens of the Wessex Saddlebacks.

Here he was momentarily flummoxed. How could you tell a Duchess from any other of several dozen Saddlebacks, most of them snoring fit to bust? Even as he thought this, a loud fruity voice rang out.

'What a perfectly ghastly row!' said the voice. 'How on earth is one expected to sleep? It is tiresome enough to have to mix with people not of one's own class, but even they, one would have thought, might have been brought up to know that it is ill-bred to snore. One wonders what in the world the Breed is coming to!'

This speech was followed by the sound of heavy bodies shifting uncomfortably, accompanied by a chorus of grunting, not all of it best pleased, as Bendigo Bung-Eye could plainly hear.

One or two voices, certainly, were apologetic, some even obsequious, their responses ranging from 'Sorry, Duchess' to 'Oh, I do beg your Grace's pardon!' But others were more outspoken.

'Who does she think she is?'

'She's not the only one who needs her beauty-sleep!'

'Calls herself a duchess – she's got no more manners than a crossbred baconer!'

'She's got a cheek, though!'

'And a big head!'

'She needs taking down a pig or two!'

While all this was going on, Bendigo made his way, walking along the tops of the wooden partitions which divided pen from pen, to the place from which the fruity voice had come. He settled himself above the large dark shape within, his front paws neatly together, his tail curled tidily around him, and considered how best to address Saddlebottom's

mother. He knew, for Sad had told him, the style which she preferred, but it seemed to him that there was nothing gracious about her, and the idea of kowtowing to her did not appeal to his proud spirit.

On the other hand he realized that he could expect no response at all, should he use such disrespectful phrases as 'Hey, you!' or 'Oi, Whatsyername!' or

'Listen to me a minute, you loud-mouthed pompous great sow!' (which is what he felt like saying).

Bendigo Bung-Eye was old and wise enough to know that compromise is usually best, so he cleared his throat and said, ''Evening, Duchess.'

He spoke loudly, and at the sound of this unfamiliar voice the other Saddlebacks ceased their grumbling and lay silent, listening.

Dorothea looked up and saw the shape of him, silhouetted against the moonlit sky outside. She gave a snort of disgust.

'One does not converse with cats,' she said.

'Name's Bung-Eye.' said Bendigo, undaunted. 'Pal of your boy.'

'My boy!' said the Duchess. 'My good animal, if you are referring to one of one's noble sons, one finds it hard to credit that Lord Henry, Lord Randolph or Lord Augustus would choose to consort with any other pig not of their own social standing, let alone a common cat.'

'Got the wrong duchess maybe,' said Bendigo. 'Pity. Looking for Duchess Dorothea. That's my pal's mum. Wanted to tell her. Great news. Great day tomorrow. For her son.'

At this several voices cut in from the surrounding darkness.

'What d'you mean, cat?'

'Tell us about the Duchess's son.'

'What's he going to do tomorrow?'

'Oh nothing much,' said Bendigo casually. 'Only be the star of this Show. Lead the parade. Meet a Royal Lady. Be in all the papers. Be on television. Be the most famous pig ever. Nothing much.'

An awed hush fell, while they all waited for the boastful remarks with which they felt sure the Duchess would greet this news. But she remained silent.

The silence was so marked that at last some bold spirit asked 'Cat got your tongue then?' but still she said nothing.

After a while Bendigo went on.

'Funny,' he said. 'He doesn't look like you.' He turned his head and cast his eye over the neighbouring pigs, all standing now in the moonlight, listening avidly to this exchange. 'Not like any of you,' he said.

'What's he look like then?' said a voice, and before Bendigo could answer, 'What's he called?' said another. 'This son of the Duchess's? What's his name? Lord What?'

'Lord nothing,' said Bendigo. 'Name's Saddlebottom.'

'Saddle*bottom*?' shouted all the listeners together.

'Yes,' said Bendigo Bung-Eye. 'He's got a white bum,' and he made his way out amidst a hubbub of delighted noise. Snorts of amusement punctuated the comments that greeted his announcement.

'Saddlebottom!'

'A white bum!!'

'Put it all behind you, Duchess!'

'There's many a slip . . .!'

'She'll never look back now!'

'She'll never hear the last of it!'

'This really is the end!'

'Jolly bad show, what, your Grace!'

'Which grace?

'Dis-grace!'

And just before he was out of earshot, Bendigo Bung-Eye heard one last voice, giving a very passable imitation of the Duchess Dorothea's haughty tones.

'One wonders,' it said, 'what in the world the Breed is coming to!'

CHAPTER 12

Mascot and Majesty

Now the great day dawned.

Promptly at 10 o'clock a large shiny Rolls Royce limousine, pennant fluttering bravely above its bonnet, drove down the central avenue of the Show Ground to the Main Ring, and to the loud applause of the huge crowd the Royal Lady stepped from it, and, accompanied by various dignitaries, made her smiling way to a specially constructed dais and took her seat.

When the cheering at last died away, there was for a moment a silence, broken only by a distant chorus of mooing, neighing, bleating and grunting. Then suddenly, dramatically, there burst upon the ears of

the spectators a great drum-roll, and into the Main Ring swept the Band of the Royal Wessex Rifles playing their regimental march, and there were not lacking among the crowd old soldiers who well remembered the words.

> 'Weeds be in the mangel-wurzels,
>   Hoe! Boys! Hoe!
> We'm the lads from Wessex,
> Where the mangel-wurzels grow.
> To keep 'em growing
> 'Tis time for hoeing,
> For everyone do know
> That the weeds be in the mangel-wurzels!
>   Hoe! Boys! Hoe!'

Up and down the Ring they marched and counter-marched, playing as they had never played before, at their head those three proud figures, the Drum-Major, the Corporal-of-Pig, and the Regimental Mascot, until at last they wheeled and came to a crashing halt before the dais.

The Bandmaster came forward and saluted, and then thousands of people at the Show Ground and millions watching on their television sets saw the Commanding Officer conduct the Royal Lady to inspect the Band of the Regiment.

Graciously she spoke to the Drum-Major, graciously she nodded at or chatted to cornettist and trombonist, euphonium-player and drummer, until at last she came to the Corporal-of-Pig and his charge, both standing, like the rest, rigidly at attention.

'What a perfectly charming pig,' said the Royal Lady, and with her parasol she gently scratched the mascot's backside, at which signal, of course, Saddlebottom immediately sat down.

'Isn't he sweet,' said the Royal Lady to the Commanding Officer. 'What's his name?'

'"Lance', Ma'am,' said the Commanding Officer.

The Royal Lady's eyes twinkled.

'Since it's such a special day,' she said, 'I think we might promote him,' and reaching forward she touched the pig between his shoulder-blades with the point of her parasol.

'Rise, Sir Lancelot,' she murmured softly.

The words meant nothing to Saddlebottom, but the touch did, and he promptly stood up and began marking time.

There was a huge roar from the watching crowd,

of surprise, of laughter, of sheer happiness, and the Royal Lady was laughing too as she returned to the dais.

And then the Band marched away behind their Regimental Mascot, and the Royal Lady had great pleasure in declaring the Show open, and the millions of people who had seen the musical parade on television spent the rest of that day saying to everyone they met, 'Did you see that fantastic pig!'

And at the end of that day, that fantastic pig, who had only got his name by courtesy of an old rat, because his mother couldn't be bothered, but who now had so many titles – '2622809 L/Cpl. Pig, W.S.' and 'Lance' and now 'Sir Lancelot' – went happily home to barracks, to be praised and made much of by everybody.

'Good boy!' said the Corporal-of-Pig, and the Bandmaster, and the Regimental Sergeant Major, and the Commanding Officer and all the other officers (except the Intelligence Officer, who said, 'Good girl!').

That evening Saddlebottom ate an enormous supper and then lay down in the deep clean straw of his quarters.

Around his neck was his collar of office. Upon his behind was his badge of rank. By his side lay his old friend, Bendigo Bung-Eye. And in his ears still was the blare of the brass and the clash of the cymbals and the boom-boom-boom of the big bass drum, until at last sweet sleep, that comes to weary warriors everywhere, crept gently up and overcame the soldier pig.

Read more in Puffin

The Sheep-Pig

by Dick King-Smith

Fly, the sheep-dog, looked at her strange new foster-child with astonishment.

The little piglet she called Babe had been won at a fair by Farmer Hogget and was surely destined to be fattened up for the family freezer, yet here he was, wanting to herd sheep! So Fly taught him everything she knew, wondering what would happen when Farmer Hogget noticed what was going on . . .

READ MORE IN PUFFIN

Dodos Are Forever

by Dick King-Smith

Beatrice and Bertie, two dodos in love, are quietly planning their future on the island paradise that is their home, and watch the ship approach with no thought of danger.

But Bertie is alarmed to realize that the newly arrived giant sea-monkeys are the enemy, and the rats they bring with them are worse still. Does this mean the end of dodos for ever? Or can a few brave birds among them pull off a daring escape?

READ MORE IN PUFFIN

For children of all ages, Puffin represents quality and variety – the very best in publishing today around the world.

For complete information about books available from Puffin – and Penguin – and how to order them, contact us at the appropriate address below. Please note that for copyright reasons the selection of books varies from country to country.

On the worldwide web: www.penguin.co.uk

In the United Kingdom: Please write to *Dept. EP, Penguin Books Ltd, Bath Road, Harmondsworth, West Drayton, Middlesex UB7 ODA*.

In the United States: Please write to *Penguin Putnam inc., P.O. Box 12289, Dept B, Newark, New Jersey 07101-5289* or call 1-800-788-6262

In Canada: Please write to *Penguin Books Canada Ltd, 10 Alcorn Avenue, Suite 300, Toronto, Ontario M4V 3B2*

In Australia: Please write to *Penguin Books Australia Ltd, P.O. Box 257, Ringwood, Victoria 3134*

In New Zealand: Please write to *Penguin Books (NZ) Ltd, Private Bag 102902, North Shore Mail Centre, Auckland 10*

In India: Please write to *Penguin Books India Pvt Ltd, 11 Panscheel Shopping Centre, Panscheel Park, New Delhi 110 017*

In the Netherlands: Please write to *Penguin Books Netherlands bv, Postbus 3507, NL-1001 AH Amsterdam*

In Germany: Please write to *Penguin Books Deutschland GmbH, Metzlerstrasse 26, 60594 Frankfurt am Main*

In Spain: Please write to *Penguin Books S. A., Bravo Murillo 19, 1° B, 28015 Madrid*

In Italy: Please write to *Penguin Italia s.r.l., Via Felice Casati 20, I–20124 Milano*

In France: Please write to *Penguin France S. A., 17 rue Lejeune, F–31000 Toulouse*

In Japan: Please write to *Penguin Books Japan, Ishikiribashi Building, 2–5–4, Suido, Bunkyo-ku, Tokyo 112*

In South Africa: Please write to *Longman Penguin Southern Africa (Pty) Ltd, Private Bag X08, Bertsham 2013*